"Jake" and other tales

Bo Shoemaker

A

Program Directors Guild

Production

Jake and other tales

Cover art by the talented Bill Smith

Editing on "Jake" by Kim R. Morse

Copyright © 2022

Published by the Program Directors Guild
Rochester, NY

Jake and other tales

Jake and other tales

To the ghosts of Keuka Lake

Jake and other tales

CONTENTS

Preface   1

Jake   3

A Solitary Plank Extending Out Into the River   27

The Derelict   32

Larry's Front Door   68

About the Author   97

Jake and other tales

Preface

These stories, written over the course of many years, are about stories, stories about stories, stories about grieving and scary things, and dark and scary things *sans* story. They are best read in a dark study (with an adequate reading lamp over your shoulder), with instrumental music playing on vinyl, a scented candle burning across the room, and with a coffee mug nearby (if in the a.m.) or a beer mug or brandy snifter nearby (if in the p.m.).

It is now 2022. Ghosts of Camp Keuka have had over a century to haunt their grounds.

Jake and other tales

"Jake"

by Bo Shoemaker; story by Brooks Parker

***

In Pennsylvania. The Alleghenies. And it wasn't just one body; it was a few.

***

If you take the federal high road south out of New York and into Pennsylvania, you'll hit the towering and creaking Alleghenies. Islets of civilization do not encroach into this wilderness—they are encroached upon. Trashy pizza-selling gas stations huddle close to the high road. *Don't go beyond me*, they seem to say. *Beyond here lies nothing.*

A dawn drive will take a traveler to a rustic-looking rest station that is perched on the highway itself. If one were to walk straight through the rest station, one would find oneself in a small circular courtyard. If the journey had begun early enough, and if the sun that day had not yet burned enough, the courtyard itself would be encircled by a wall of Pennsylvania mountain fog. As the fog cleared, one would see that the courtyard is actually on the precipice of a cliff. The cliff overlooks the Tioga reservoir hundreds of feet below, pristinely perfect in its artificiality. The high road crosses the reservoir in an impressive bridge reflective of the industry of which man is capable. But none of those men had stuck around. They came along, built the high road, sweat and struggled and camped to build the colossal bridge, and left and never returned. The bridge remained. The reservoir remained. The mountains remained.

A little further south, past Mansfield University, skirting the village of Liberty, one begins to see signs for Cogan House.

"That's just the name of the town," Tristan clarified. He was hunched over a rustic wooden table, his eyes level with the top of a pint glass of bock. He squinted and a smile, informed by the first two beers, appeared. "The summerhouse is a little bit past, in the state game lands." He took a big gulp. "I have it for all of August. Plenty of rooms." It was to be a veritable hotel through the month, with travelers, students, and professionals coming and going. Tristan would be the host through it all. Halfway through that third bock, a rudimentary map was drawn on a sturdy napkin retrieved from atop the bar. In it, a windy black line shot out from the high road, took some twists and turns, and ended at a small doodle of a house—the summerhouse. It was nestled near a peak labeled "Billy's Bald Top."

Tristan was a hopeless graduate student at the university. His master's program seemed never-ending—doors continually opening and closing, revealing new and meandering corridors in his labyrinthine education. The summer stay in the cabin would be yet another excuse to string out his length of time before attainment of degree.

The first person went missing at a party around the middle of August. Dozens of cars had crammed into the tiny lot in front of Tristan's vacation house. The downstairs rooms were full of mingling partygoers—some graduate students from Mansfield, the odd undergraduate, some friends of Tristan's from back home, and some hangers-on. The music thudded loudly. Conversation was nigh-impossible. It was that kind of party. In the small hours of the morning, when things began to wind down, one of the girls suddenly realized that she was missing her companion. The upstairs rooms, reserved for spur-of-the-moment assignations, were checked to no avail. The yard and outbuildings were likewise empty of the partygoer in question.

Her friend, now becoming more distraught, retraced the evening, along with Tristan, myself, the few guests who remained, and others we were able to raise by phone or text message. The missing girl had been present in the house through midnight: Some outdoors revelers had seen her near the rake shed, toward the back of the yard, shortly after that. After midnight, there had been no notice of her.

We went to the rake shed. It stood alone at the edge of the yard, where the vague boundary between tamed lawn and coniferous forest began to tilt toward the latter. I remember looking up in those pre-dawn moments; the trees towered over the shed, the house, the yard, the cars. And the trees went on and on, a metropolis. At the small area beyond the yard began the familiar arboreal neighborhood. But it took only a moment to realize that there were hundreds, thousands of neighborhoods like this that stretched along this side of the mountain, around it, and across the other side.

State police cars came and went. The search got underway shortly after sunup, and Tristan's house became the base of operations. He and I hadn't known the girl, but we felt it was our duty to help however we could. Coffee, toaster pastries, and even eggs were on the menu for many of the police searchers.

Come afternoon, when there was still no sign of the girl, civilians from Cogan House and Liberty, as well as some summer students from Mansfield, began gathering in the yard for an arm-in-arm-style search walk.

Up Billy's Bald Top we went, trudging through the seasons-old leaves and over fallen logs to where quiet reigned. Snaps and shuffles announced our presence. Chirps and tweets were returned. Deer cleared off.

Finally, when we were about three-fourths of the way to the top of the peak, we heard shouting coming from near the center of the line. They had found something. By the time we got there the state police were trying to keep everybody back, but they lacked the manpower. I tried peering around the troopers to see what may lie on the ground, but I saw nothing of note. Then Tristan pointed up to the pine canopy.

At first it was unclear exactly what it was I was seeing, the sight was so out of context. It looked like jungle moss draping down toward the ground. Then it became apparent that the jungle moss was actually hair. That the white pieces of what had appeared to be bark or other matter were, in fact, fingernails that had grown preternaturally long. A body was strung up by its ankles. The skin was gone. The blood was dried.

The state police finally coaxed everyone to a dignified distance before cutting the body down. There was no way this could be the missing girl, some said. We'd be back searching the next day, said others. But we weren't.

The Tioga *Freedomist* was rife with yellow journalism the next morning. The girl had, apparently, been identified through her dental records. Questions were aplenty: To where with her skin? Why and how were her hair and fingernails? By whom? And buried in one of the back pages was an opinion piece by a Cogan House contributor, titled: "Jake Returns?"

Jake was, apparently, an old hermit who lived at the eponymous clearing at the peak of Billy's Bald Top. No roads went up that far—only hiking paths. And rare was the traveler who came upon Jake's enclosure. The Old Logger's Road went about halfway up the far side of the mountain, and it was at its end that an unlucky clerk from the local convenience brought Jake his deliveries. The method of payment was a matter of rumor and speculation—perhaps cash, perhaps animal skins, perhaps barter goods. Over the years, some hikers had returned to Mansfield with tales of a strange little shack nestled in the Bald Top, but none had seen the man himself. Only eerie silence, or, in one or two cases, startling, unknowable sounds that sent them hustling back down the trail.

Jake was not taken seriously by those who believed themselves to be serious, of course. He was a spook story. Or, at most, he was just a recluse, one step away from a homeless. Maybe the "shanty" was no more than cardboard boxes snatched from local cabins or from behind local restaurants, held together with some sticks and twine. Or maybe there wasn't really a

Jake at all—maybe different tramps had played the part from year to year.

Tristan had taken a keen interest in the Jake story, however, and decided to meet with the enigmatic columnist while I watched over the summerhouse. For hours he was gone, and for hours past his appointed time of return.

Night came on. The wind ceased. Some kind of nut had already begun falling from the trees, and every so often a small thud would resound through the atrium of the house. Finally, around 3 a.m., headlights swung through the living room. Tristan strode inside without looking at me. He had some people with him. "Get some sleep," he ordered, apparently toward everyone else in the room, myself included. "We'll leave at sunup." Then Tristan and a short, rotund, bearded, balding man began taking inventory of the house and of several bags that the man began retrieving from the car. I recognized the face of this man, though only barely. His younger, thinner, cleaner visage had appeared in the by-line of the Jake column in the *Freedomist.*

Through the floor of one of the upstairs rooms, as I drifted in and out of sleep, I heard Tristan and the columnist planning routes, separating us into teams, preparing, preparing, preparing. There appeared to be no speculation as to who or what Jake was—that had already been taken care of in the offices (or the tiny home?) of the columnist. Tristan had already been convinced, as had the few graduate students he had persuaded to come along.

After some hours, a thrumming energy in the house caused me to awaken. Everyone was assembling and gearing up. A dull grey light came through the window. When I stood to look out, I found that I could already begin to see the evergreens at the far end of the yard. They didn't look foreboding. They didn't look inviting. They were just there.

We set out, after quick coffee and breakfast, with packs on each of our backs. We each had a rather detailed map of Billy's Bald Top, complete with elevation, trails, and a black star where Jake's shack was supposedly located. Two groups of three were to search. One was to follow the girl's supposed trail along a well-trodden hiking path through the woods while the other group—my group—made a beeline for where the girl was ultimately found. There this group would attempt to discern whether she had come from the summerhouse to here, whether she had come from the shack to here, or whether her trail had been something less logical than Tristan and the columnist had anticipated.

Police tape still lay beneath the girl's final perch. The ground had been pretty well swept clean of her property and biological material. Along with a forestry student, Tristan and I spread around the spot, trying to make note of anything that would explain how the girl here came and how she had been strung up so high. About an hour into this investigation, I found myself scaling one of the sturdier-looking trees, close behind the forestry student. Tristan belayed us from the ground.

"Hello," the forestry student murmured, reaching out for something. He yanked at what, to me, appeared to be only a cluster of twigs, cones, and pine brushes. He must have seen my puzzlement, for he soon turned to me with open hand. Atop his palm, at about the same size, was a primitive looking pulley.

Back on the ground, we studied the pulley some more. The pine needles lodged inside it were still freshly green. "This is how he got her up there," Tristan concluded. The forestry student nodded.

Noon came and went. The other party did not come. Nor could we raise them with cellular or satellite technology. Once we all consumed cheese, crackers, and sugary syrup, Tristan determined that we would set out for the summit. There we could learn more on our own, and perhaps would meet the other team along the way.

The going became slower and slower as we neared the peak. Trails became more difficult to spot. The elevation became more treacherous. Two or three times, I or Tristan stumbled and, luckily, caught onto a tree, limiting our slip down the embankment to only a couple dozen feet.

Finally, after much sweat and effort (and boot-tightening on my part, for I had not anticipated so strenuous a climb), we espied the little grotto that comprised the Bald Top. Across the field, I could barely make out a small shack and a somewhat smaller outbuilding near to it. Tristan held up his hand and we took cover behind trees, logs, and leaves. There we waited.

There was the sound of birds, but they all seemed so far off. A pair of squirrels fought high above my head. One of them fell some feet from me and, like a Tex Avery character, sprung back up, wily as ever, and scurried away.

Still we waited. Thirty minutes went by. The other team did not arrive. The other team did not answer when Tristan surreptitiously attempted to call them. Nothing moved in the clearing.

A wind came. It drowned out the sound of my ticking watch, which had begun to set my nerves on end. From across the grove came the sound of an atonal wind chime, though I knew that it was not the usual tubes of metal or wood that played this Partch-like étude.

The wind left. The strange resonance ceased. The sun began to edge closer to a nearby peak. We would soon find ourselves in a short-lived twilight. Tristan decided to move. The three of us marched, in line, into the glade, machetes and hunting knives unsheathed and at the ready. We mounted a grass-covered knoll of about fifty yards across that gave way to a steep slope, like the side of a sand trap, more toward the shack than not. From this little ridge we were some feet above the shack and its outbuilding. The buildings faced each other with a little dirt lane worn out in between.

We waited some minutes more. There was no sign of movement from the grove, from the woods, or from the buildings.

We slid down the sandy slope one at a time. Tristan signaled the forestry student to keep watch from the outside. He signaled me toward the outbuilding. Tristan headed to the shack. The shack was not made of cardboard, after all. It was a log cabin: The windows were squares cut out of the wall with no glass or plastic covering them. He peered into one of the windows and I turned my attention to the outbuilding.

The outbuilding was, too, made of wood. But its sides were smooth—more like a gingerbread house than Lincoln Logs. It had no windows. It was slightly elevated from the ground so there was a foot or so of space underneath its floor. Stone or concrete columns seemed to hold it up, and a wide, flat stone step led up to a brown sliding door.

I approached and waited. I tested the door. It slid to the left rather easily, with no sound. I aimed my light into the opening and noticed that, due to imperfections in the seal on the opposite wall, light shone into the small room despite the lack of windows. I pulled the door aside some more and stepped in. Hanging from the ceiling in an irregular array were dozens of blades. They came in seemingly all shapes and sizes: flat, jagged, curved, one-sided, two-sided, four-sided. I could not completely make out some of the more peculiar-looking blades on the far side of the room; they were concealed by their more ordinary brothers, and by the darkness.

I heard fingers snapping from outside. I turned and left the outbuilding. When I closed the door, its runners made a little low-pitched squeaking sound.

Tristan was closing the door to the shack. The forestry student looked expectantly over to Tristan—apparently the latter had done the snapping. We met in the worn path between the two buildings. I suppose I might have looked anxious or afeared, for Tristan asked, "What's in there?"

"Blades," I whispered. "Lots of blades."

Tristan nodded, "Chemicals in mason jars in there." That is all I would ever learn about what was inside the cabin. He waited a moment, listening, hearing nothing. "Let's get out of here. Right now."

We padded along the path and into the woods, now across the clearing from the way we had come.

We saw the other team almost immediately. They were up high in the trees but, because of where we stood on the sloping mountain, they were almost at eye-level. All three hung, upside-down, by their ankles. Their fingernails were feet, *feet*, long. Their hair was so long it nearly touched the ground. All were without their skins. Their backpacks and other items were nowhere to be seen. The forestry student and I gasped. Tristan seemed too shocked to make a noise.

But our stillness lasted only a moment. From behind us we heard the same low-pitched squeak that I had heard moments before. Only this time, there was something purposeful, deliberate about the movement of the door that we now heard. This was not the sound of a tentative trespasser maneuvering the door – the only person who would close it with such confidence, with such carelessness of the utterance it would make in this still and foreboding wood, was its owner.

We began scampering down the steep forest trail before we could hear the branches snapping behind us that would have announced Jake's approach. We made it to the summerhouse as the evening was nearing its end. By now it was night in the woods, but in the yard of the house some light yet remained. Tristan threw his pack in his car. The forestry student and I jumped in. There would be time later, much later, to come back for our things in the house. The imperative at this moment was to get away, far away, fast.

There would be no phone call, not even an anonymous one. Three more were now missing. Three more would be found.

Tristan's summer vacation on Billy's Bald Top ended when his car spun around in the small lot in front of the summerhouse and sped out the driveway and down the mountain, spewing dirt and gravel

behind it.

A Solitary Plank Extending Out Into the River

A solitary plank extending out into the river, while down south there were docks and visitors and the lights of cities and villages. Here, it was dark and rural. The plank connected the boat to the shore, where there was a slight dirt path cutting and winding through the black and green wood. Mist slothed along the ground. Out there, beyond the tree line, were unknowns. Bustling civilization not to be found here. No security at night, when all aboard the boat were asleep, either in the main cabin or on the deck. There were animals and crickets there on shore. Did something move? A shadow among shadows.

Somewhere far off, far off, there was a dog quietly baying. Just near the point where the lapping waves of the Hudson could no longer be heard, he was baying. He paced and paced in the little mud room of the shack. The shack in a small clearing in the wood. High above, a quiet and persistent moon. The clearing was bluegreen in the light and the trees whispered. The dog paused again and stared. Then he barked once more. Off at the edge of the trees something moved. Something beckoned.

Back in the dark of the shack was a bed. In the bed was the man. The man had a red beard and a red mustache. He had a baseball hat on. Even with his eyes closed, he had the look of staring off into the distance. Never being quite there. He was always like that, but looked especially so now. Even with his eyes closed. He was having a dream of a just-now-remembered thing. He'd been a boy vacationing in Hawaii. Or was it Florida? He and his parents went to an early-bird breakfast. The building was all white and glass. The sun was already high, bright, and hot. They sat in large tables, several families to a table. Early-bird. He definitely remembered it was early-bird. With one of the families was another young boy like him. Or was it a girl? But he or she was definitely in the company of an old woman. Very old. Impossibly ancient. Her wrinkles were overdone, really. She was in a wheelchair, and had trouble speaking. She had trouble walking too, apparently. And the man remembered that she'd had trouble eating or talking. She was too old, he thought as a boy. And he remembered shaking his head to himself, about her. And he clucked his tongue to himself, about her. She was too old. She should not have been so old. Now. Now. Now he was a man. The woman was certainly dead. His father was old. But not, not, not too old. Or would some little boy or girl somewhere say that he *was*?

A good ways down the driveway of the shack was a gravel road. A good ways down the gravel road was an abandoned salt mine. And near the salt mine there's this old phone booth. It's like red around the sides, and plastic, not like a british phone booth. It just has like two red fins on the side. And a 70's style bubble on top. Behind the phone booth is a gate, and a gate house (no one's inside though). Behind that are these two silos, but they have corners. Like two Lego pieces. Square shaped silos. Square shaped silos. Sometimes in the middle of the night, when no one is around, the pay phone rings. No one is around to answer it, so it rings and rings for like 5 or 10 minutes, then stops. One time a guy was out riding his trail bike and he heard it ringing, so he rode over towards the ringing noise to check out what the ringing noise was. He saw square shaped silos against the midnight black sky, trees in foreground. The fence was rusty and when the wind blew, little metal signs would *clink* and *clatter* against it, like a happy maraca of death. Or rumba shakers, if you will. Square shaped silos got closer and closer. The phone was ringing. They found him a month later

The Derelict

***

Thunder clapped, almost immediately upon us, and we began jogging away from the forest. About halfway across the field the sky opened up, and the six of us burst in the building with our jackets dripping and our socks soaked. The Dining Hall, perched on a precipice overlooking tumultuous Lake Ontario, shook and creaked from the wind of the newly arrived storm.

I had come to Camp Keenan for a conference of area camp directors. Mark Dibble and I represented Camp Keuka, there were two men there representing a camp from out near Buffalo, and then there was Jack, the Director of Keenan itself.

The wind groaned around the building, and Jack got one of his staff to make a fire. We warmed ourselves while the staff member ran over to an adjoining building for spare shirts and socks. We watched while, outside, the skies over Lake Ontario become ever darker, disguising mid-day as dusk.

"This reminds me," said one of the Buffalo directors, "of a storm we had at our camp once. It was night, and everyone was stuck in the cabins; the rain just wouldn't let up. One of the 12-year-old kids starts screaming to his counselor that he sees a face outside his window. We kept trying to tell him that his window was 15 feet off the ground but he swore he saw a face. Then a bunch of kids all up and down that row of cabins started screaming that they saw a face, too. The counselors had a meeting outside on a porch, and the kids wouldn't let them back in the cabin, they were so scared. The counselors had to break in through a window to get back inside. Then finally the storm passes and I start talking to the counselors over there. Turns out the village director had told a scary story at the campfire that night, and that was what got the kids all scared."

"Do you allow scary stories at your camp?" I asked.

"Sure, unless it goes overboard. A little scary story at a campfire is fine now and then; it's what camp is about."

I was curious, "What was this scary story about? The one the village director told to the kids."

"It was something called *H-Man*."

"We have that one," I said.[1]

____

[1] *See* Shoemaker, *A History of Camp Keuka*(Charleston: History Press, 2011), 52.

Jake and other tales

"About the guy with the fire in his cabin, and he tries to get through the gated window and it burns an 'H' into his chest?"

I nodded, "Sounds pretty much the same. You guys have any stories particular to your camps that you tell a lot? Scary stories?"

Jack said that his camp told a version of *The Man with the Golden Arm*, and also a story about a C.I.T. who was left out in the woods with two matches to see if he could make it through the night. According to the story, he was never seen again, and only one spent match was found in a clearing the next day. "But the scariest thing that ever happened to me at this camp was when I was a Village Director," Jack said. "It was preseason and our maintenance guy, a guy who'd worked here for forty years, took us all around the camp on a tour. He told us the story of the C.I.T. in the woods, and then that night while we were all in bed we heard these noises out in the forest. None of us knew what they were, but we were all too scared to go look. It was like cracking, like trees were being broken in half. Then there was all this banging on the windows downstairs from where we were staying. Banging at every window, really fast. We all got really scared then, we being just these half dozen college kids out here in the middle of nowhere. We called the police, and they said they'd send a car, but we never saw one, and we never heard anything back." He laughed, "I don't think any of us got to sleep that night. Next morning we go out into the woods and see that someone had made a big bonfire that was, by now, all burned out, but we never figured out who."

We all got quiet for a minute, thinking about our own frightening moments. Rain whipped outside, and the dark waves kept pounding against the concrete platforms that inexplicably extended a dozen yards out into the lake, at regular intervals, like splayed fingers on black silk.

"Something happened to me when I visited Camp Keuka last summer," I finally spoke up.

***

On July 4, I decided to take a break from studying for the Bar and drove down to camp, watching the fireworks with the staff. During Keuka Lake's Independence Day celebrations, all of the boaters drive up the lake to the Village of Penn Yan so they can watch the fireworks. Once the fireworks are over, there's a mass exodus of boats – you never see anything like it the rest of the summer.

Over a hundred boats hurtle, right to left, down the lake from the Village. From the rocky beach at camp, it appears that the lake is full of balls of lights, all moving at different speeds. Then there are stragglers, so that by 10:30 or 11:00 a boat's driving by every few minutes or so. Usually, by midnight, there are no more boats out there; they've all made it home.

I was in the Office building, reading through some old camp documents. Adam, our Director of Sailing, was on Claw that night, so he was in the building too. Claw is what we call our Night Watch. He left the building at midnight to do his walkthrough, and he came back after a few minutes. He said there was a big boat just sitting out in the middle of the lake.

I weighted my papers down with an encyclopedia volume and left the building with him to head down to the beach. I could see something out there in the middle of the lake, but there were no lights on it, and our flashlights couldn't reach that far. I could tell it was a big outline of something, but that's about all I could tell. So we woke up Mark, and he said to go check it out. Adam went over to the office to get some radios so we could communicate with Mark back on shore. His cabin looks out over the lake; he would be able to see us from his windows.

While Mark and I waited in his cottage for Adam, Mark said that when he'd woken up to see Adam and myself standing over his bed, it had reminded him of another time, when he had been a young counselor, that he had been woken up in the middle of the night. Mark said that he'd heard someone walking around in the cabin down on the waterfront, and had woken up to see a face over his bed. Standing there had been a small person with a large, almost impossibly large, head. Mark hadn't wanted want the man, or whatever it was, to know that Mark was awake, so he'd pretended to be asleep, and eventually the man had left the cabin. Mark had been too afraid to follow.

Once Mark finished telling me this story, Adam returned, and the two of us left Mark's cottage. Adam and I grabbed lifejackets and took the party boat out towards the middle of the lake. As we got closer, I could see that the boat out there was actually a two-story boat. Then the moon came out from behind a cloud, and a streak of silver shot down across the water so that I could see the boat even better.

It's the *Viking Spirit*, a big behemoth of a ship, like a giant black parallelogram with orange piping. The boat was a really ugly thing, and was to have been retired at the end of that summer. We usually saw it going past the camp once a week or so. It had been on Keuka Lake for years, possibly decades. It was meant as a sort of throwback to the lake's heyday, when the economy was booming and wealthy tourists packed the shores every summer. More recently, it carried low-income weekenders looking for a low-cost vacation.

We radioed back to Mark what we saw, but we couldn't see if there were any people on board. Adam and I were a little afraid to call out across the water, so we cut the engines and pulled up alongside the big boat. Adam tied us on, and we just sat there on the party boat for a few minutes, trying to get up our nerve, thinking that maybe we should board the ship to check it out. Adam finally said, "This is pretty creepy, huh?" I nodded back. He asked, "Is this the creepiest thing you've ever done here?"

I thought about it for a minute, then said, "Done, maybe, but this isn't the most *scared* I've ever been at camp."

"When was that?" Adam asked.

"Probably my very first week here ever, when I was twelve. I had this counselor, Brooks, and one night instead of having a devotional he just told us a scary story while we were all in our beds." I smiled, "I remember at one point I had to cover my ears because I was so scared."

Adam was intrigued, "What was the story was about, if you remember?" The party boat rocked on the dark water, little *plops* of waves striking the pontoon.

I did remember; that story had had a big impact on me. I'd written it down immediately after returning home from camp, and I had even tried re-telling it a few times over the years, but I could never quite get the mood that I remembered feeling that night in that cabin when I was twelve.

"It was about this guy, Jake, a hermit. He lived on top of this mountain called Billy's Bald Top, which I'm not sure is actually real. Anyway, he was just this creepy guy; he paid someone in town to deliver groceries to someplace near the foot of the mountain every so often. No one ever really saw him, but they knew he had some shack up at the summit. In the story, there's a group of college kids, I think, who have a house halfway up the mountain. They're having a party, and one of the girls goes missing. They don't really realize it at first, and then as the party's winding down they realize she's been gone for hours.

"So they all go out looking for her in the woods on the side of the mountain but they don't find her. The next day the sheriff gets together a search party, and a bunch of the college kids from the house help out. They form a big line and start walking up through the mountain woods. Pretty soon one of them spots something up in a tree. It's a human body, but all the skin's gone, and the hair and fingernails are super-long, like they'd been growing for months and months. They cut it down, and they can tell by dental records that it's the missing girl from the party. Then they realize that someone from the search party had just gone missing in the last few minutes.

"This was the part of the story where I covered my ears for a few minutes, so I'm not sure what happens next, but eventually there's a smaller search party going up to the top of the hill to talk to Jake. They get to the top of the hill, where there's this bald top, a big open space, and they see this shack kind of tucked into a crevice. They go inside and see all sorts of carving instruments, blades, saws, hanging from the ceiling. But Jake's not there. Then they all run out of the shack and leave the mountain forever. Somewhere in there they found the missing search party guy, hanging from a tree, skinned, long hair and fingernails, just like the girl. But I can't remember if that's before or after they find the shack.

"Imagine you're a twelve-year-old kid at an overnight camp for the first time, hearing that. I was terrified." I waited a minute, "I don't think we're doing a very good job of getting our courage up."

We radioed Mark, who was still back in his cabin. He agreed that we should go on board the boat to check it out, but to be careful. In the meantime, he would wake up a counselor to sit on the porch of the Yacht Club to keep watch on us with binoculars. If anyone saw anything too weird, Mark or the counselor would call the sheriff.

Adam and I checked our flashlights, then Adam said, "An alumnus was here dropping off his kids at the beginning of the week, and he told me about this thing he saw here at night one time."

"Yeah? What was it?" I walked over to the railing of the party boat, preparing to climb over.

"He said when he was on Claw, back in the '80s, he saw a man running through camp. You know, like jogging. He followed the guy to see who it was – the guy was running over towards one of the bridges into Senior Village, and he heard the banging on the bridge from the guy's feet. But then the footsteps stopped before they should have, about halfway across the bridge. Chris went over to the bridge but there was no one there, and no one in the creek below."

"Did he ever find out anything else about it?" I asked.

"No," Adam looked down in disappointment, seeming a little ashamed that he'd brought up a story with no resolution.

"It seems like that kind of stuff happens a lot," I reassured him. "You know, something scary, never really explained. You could think it's real, like a real ghost, or just some trick your mind played on you, or you could figure it's just a neighbor going for a jog at night, and the wind or something covered up the rest of his footsteps and he ran off camp. Can't know everything, I guess."

"Yeah, I guess," Adam walked over to join me at the railing.

"Like one time," I began, "this new counselor comes to me one morning around the beginning of the summer and says, 'Can I ask you something and not get a bullshit answer?' I said sure. He goes, 'Is the Dining Hall haunted?' I guess he thought that I, as Camp Historian, would know for sure. He'd gone in there the night before and when he'd opened the door he'd seen something running through the Dining Hall. I tried to tell him it was probably just the light reflecting off of the door as he opened it, but he was sure that couldn't be it—he'd tried to re-create his entrance into the building and didn't see the same thing again. I believe it was a trick of the light, a reflection, or a squirrel or something. But I'm pretty sure he still thinks it was a ghost." I smiled.

Then I reached over for the big wooden railing on the *Viking Spirit* and pulled myself aboard. Adam followed, and we both stopped for a minute. We were on a small, carpeted platform, like a front porch for the big boat. We looked over to the Party Boat, which we had just left. Camp Territory. We looked at our immediate surroundings on the outer deck of the

Viking Spirit—foreign territory. Adam shined his flashlight into the main cabin, but couldn't see much. It looked like there were some tables or benches in there, but his flashlight couldn't penetrate the tinted window enough to show any detail. We would have to go in. We radioed Mark first, to tell him our plan. He said to go for it.

I opened the big wooden door into the cabin, and, slowly, we both entered. The place was dead quiet. All of the natural sounds of the outside were muted. We were enclosed. Benches lined the room like pews, and we started walking up the aisle, moving our flashlights around to see if there was anything, or anyone, there. All of the emergency life jackets were still in their cubbies, and there was no evidence that anything peculiar had happened. A few pieces of luggage were scattered about—backpacks and purses, mostly—but other than that, nothing. There were a few light switches, but nothing happened when we flipped them—we figured the power must be controlled from the bridge, up on the second floor.

The crackle of the radio startled the two of us; it was Mark. "Hey guys, I just saw something, can you see the boardwalk from where you are?"

I looked across the lake towards camp. Something caught my eye, something far away. I told Adam to turn off his light. He protested at first, but relented after a moment. Once it was dark in the cabin, I tried to focus on the shore at camp. There was a man, clad in all white, walking down the boardwalk along the shore. He vanished into some trees.

"What did you see?" I asked over the radio.

"It was a guy walking down the beach, towards the boardwalk," Mark related. "It looked like he was wearing an old staff uniform like they used to wear in the '20s. I tried calling out to him, but he kept walking. When I got out of my cabin to follow him I couldn't see him anymore."

"What's going on here?" Adam asked.

"I don't know," I said. The boat rocked back and forth gently. The moon glimmered on the water before another cloud passed overhead, darkening the reflection. "You good to keep going?" I asked, and he nodded.

"You know," I said, "I just remembered a couple other times at camp I was as afraid as right now, or almost as afraid." Here I was trying to stoke courage in both of us. "One time, a few years ago, I was on Claw, in the store past midnight. A car came rolling up to the parking lot, and a big, strong-looking man got out. I was very scared, but only for a second, that he was a murderer or kidnapper. He walked towards the back of the store, where I was sitting, and asked me if he could have a campsite for the night. Apparently there's some tourist map that shows our camp as a campground, not as a summer camp for children. I explained the error to the man and directed him to Camp Wigwam on the other side of the lake. He walked out of the store—he didn't know that the whole time we'd been talking my arm was hidden behind a door with a baton, ready to slam the door into him and/or hit him with the baton if he turned out to be a psycho."

"What was the other time?" Adam asked. "The other time that you were as scared as now?"

I smiled, "It was when I was a C.I.T. We were getting ready to go to bed, all in our cabins up on the hill. We were just about to turn off the light in the cabin when we heard this voice out in the middle of the field, going 'Boo-lah!' or something. Dave, our Leadership Director, came running up the hill from the office, shouting at all of us to get into one cabin. We all did, and one counselor watched us while a half dozen or so other staff members chased the interlopers around camp. At one point we thought that maybe someone was hiding around the back of the cabin, so the counselor walked around to check. When she came back around to the front door this guy Rob and I were standing there with a broom and a guitar, ready to use them as weapons. The interlopers ended up escaping, and a few days later we discovered that it was the boyfriend of this girl in our group, and his friends.

"In order to cheer us all up after that night, Dave told us a story of something he did when he was a younger counselor. Back then one person would sit in the middle of the village and watch all the cabins from ten to midnight, so every counselor had a night off almost every night. Anyway, the girl who was watching the village that night was kind of passive and weak-willed, and Dave's cabin of older boys was kind of rowdy, so Dave and his co-counselor assured her that they'd make sure the boys were quiet. Around 10:15, Dave and his co went into the cabin and told the boys, 'Some of the other staff saw a man in the ravine, with a rope.' They told the kids they didn't know who he was or why he was at camp, not to be alarmed, but to be quiet, or else the man might come over towards the cabin. Dave and his co came back to the cabin every twenty minutes or so with updates, 'He was seen over by the Chapel, we don't know, maybe he left camp,' or 'He was seen right outside this cabin.' Around eleven, Dave stopped and enjoyed the rest of his time off. Right before midnight, as he was coming back to the cabin, he saw that several of the beds were empty. He and his co began to get worried, until they shined their flashlights on one of the top bunks, in the corner. There, all these big, tough 15-year-olds were huddled together on the same bunk, under a blanket."

Adam was smiling a little now; we were ready to continue on. He turned to me, "What about that thing about the Bluff Point Stoneworks?"

I started walking towards the other end of the room, "I do not want to talk about that."

Adam and I opened the wooden door leading to the staircase. We started taking the steps up and were about to the landing when our radios crackled. It was Mark: "Did you guys happen to call the sheriff on your cell phones already?" I touched my pocket, felt that it was empty and realized that I had left my phone on the party boat.

"No, why?" I asked

"Someone was just knocking on my door, and I thought it might have been because you called someone."

"No, we didn't. Who was it?"

Mark: "I'm not sure; no one was there when I opened the door."

There was a pause.

Then Adam told Mark that he and I were going up to the *Viking Spirit*'s wheelhouse, to see if we could get the power on, or to see if we could find anything up there. Mark acknowledged.

The stairs brought us out onto a big, open deck. The moon, the wind, and the sound of the waves were back. Far away on shore, a big 18-wheeler went over a bump in the road. That familiar *thunk, thunk!*

The wheelhouse was on the far side of the deck, at the front of the ship. A strong-looking wooden door, with a single tiny window in it, led to the wheelhouse. We could not see inside the room from where we were—the walls were solid, possibly to avoid any revelers distracting the pilot when the ship was underway. There were benches up here on deck, and on one of them Adam found two sticks for shooting off fireworks. One of them had been fired; one hadn't. We walked the rest of the way down the deck, opened the wooden door to the wheelhouse, and stepped inside, once again shutting out the mere.

Once in the wheelhouse we could see that the ignition key was gone, but Adam thought there would be a separate switch for the power. Only by turning off our flashlights and seeing a red LED indicator could we find the switch. But before Adam could flip it, we heard a rapping at the wooden wheelhouse door, and we both froze, holding our breaths.

The boat rocked back and forth – the wind was picking up a little. Adam began to whisper, "Maybe something rolled against the wall downstairs-" but I raised my hand to shut him up.

We waited a few moments more, and there was no sound. Then, *knock, knock, knock*, on the door to the wheelhouse. Adam and I were frozen—we had looked through almost the entire boat, seeing no one. Now there was no mistaking the sound: some person was definitely knocking on the door to the room in which we now stood. From our position we could not see the window on the door. Neither of us moved for a moment, but then Adam moved towards the door. "Wait-" I tried to say, but he already opened it.

I looked over with him, turning on my flashlight. There was nothing but an empty deck. Yet we had certainly not given time enough for a person to have made it to the stairs. Adam and I went back into the wheelhouse, closing the door behind us, and latching it.

Adam flipped the power switch, and running lights came on alongside the exterior rim of the ship.

Then *Bam! Bam! Bam!* shook the door.

Adam and I huddled in the corner, hoping the latch would hold if something tried to get through. I whispered urgently at the radio, "Mark, Mark, there's someone *on the boat with us!*" Mark spoke softly back that he was calling the sheriff.

Minutes passed, Adam and I waiting in the wheelhouse. There had been no noises of any kind since I had last radioed Mark. Then the cabin filled with light. A spotlight down on the water was shining up at us. Adam and I stood, looking out the giant window, and saw the Yates County Sheriff boat down there.

"You boys alright?" The driver called to us. I gave him a thumbs-up. "Stay there; we're sending someone up to you," he said, and another sheriff's deputy hopped onto the lower deck of the *Viking Spirit*.

The deputy found us and walked us back through the boat, which was now well-lit by police spotlight, plus the overhead lights we had flipped on. Shadows shot across the enclosed lower deck as the spotlight followed us. For a split-second I thought I saw something human-shaped, crouching in the corner. But I looked a moment too long, and then it was gone.

"It was pretty stupid of you boys to come out here alone," the deputy was scolding. "You should have called us once you saw a derelict on the lake." I nodded, still a little shaken, and apologized. Adam and I got back onto the party boat and drove back to the Y-dock at camp. To drive the several hundred yards across the water back to camp was to drive between worlds. Mark was there to meet us.

"Fun night, huh?" He asked, smiling.

"Yeah," I grinned, feeling better now that I was back at camp, and off that boat. The three of us started walking off the dock. "I wonder," I said, "if we'll ever find out why the *Viking Spirit* was out there tonight, abandoned."

Mark shrugged, looking up at the mostly-hidden stars. "Seems like all the real ghost stories don't have endings."

I sighed, "Or a lot of them aren't even stories."

Mark agreed, "Like when Ben Gilberg swore he saw that werewolf, or alien, or whatever he said it was, on the porch of his cabin back in the '90s. People talked about it for a while, but, no story, just Ben claiming that he saw it."

"Or when Dave was on claw, and he thought he was following campers around in the dark." I added.

"I haven't heard that one," Mark prodded.

"Oh!" I was glad for a chance to tell something lighthearted. "Dave was crawling around camp in the dark, not turning on his flashlight or anything, because he thought he was following campers who were trying to sneak out. He kept hearing the twigs crack from what he assumed were campers' footfalls. Finally he thought he had them cornered under the Senior Boathouse, so he turned on the flashlight and got ready to yell at them. But instead of campers he saw a giant muskrat – a huge one! So he screamed and ran back to the store." Adam, Mark, and I all laughed. Then Mark and I said goodnight to Adam, who went into the Yacht Club to sleep. It was now past 1 am.

Mark and I went up the hill—he towards his cottage and I towards the store building. I was sleeping on Mark's couch that night, but I didn't want to leave my historical documents where they were, near an open window. A breeze was blowing in what felt like a damp chill, and I thought this forebode rain later on in the night.

I picked up the documents, tucked them under my arm, and headed back out into the blackness. Then I heard gravel shifting underfoot from over on my right, in Senior Village. I saw a person, probably a man, walking away from me, across the field. He was wearing what looked to be a white shirt, with white pants tucked into high socks, like the staff used to wear in Camp Keuka's first decades. The man approached a cabin, walked across the porch, and insouciantly opened the door and walked in, closing the door behind him with a *splish*.

I jogged across the field, my eyes never leaving that cabin. I got up to the door, opened it, and looked inside. Through the dark, I could see the children and counselors asleep in their beds. I shined my flashlight all over the cabin, looking for the intruder, but I saw nothing. There was no trace of the man I had seen.

I hurried outside and sprinted back through the night, towards Mark's cottage.

***

By now the storm at Camp Keenan had almost passed. We changed back into our clothes, which had sufficiently dried by the fire, and had a quick bite to eat before we headed back to our homes. Mark and I got into his car and drove out Camp Keenan's long driveway. We left that world, which was all its own, with all its own myths and mysteries that we could never hope to fully comprehend.

"Larry's Front Door"

We were in one of the patient rooms up on the sixth floor and all of the lights were dim. It was night outside. Out there, down at street level, people were walking, eating, drinking. Up here it was quiet except for the noise of the machinery and the sound of a patient care tech coming in every 30 minutes or so to check on my dad's vitals.

By now he was pretty much asleep in bed. I had pulled two chairs together to make a little recliner for myself, and we were watching *The Big Lebowski* on his laptop. A movie every few nights, half of the movie at a time. We'd made our way through *This is Spinal Tap* and *Monty Python and the Holy Grail*.

We'd gotten about to the halfway point of *Lebowski* and I got up to turn it off. We'd finish it on

Friday, probably. My dad awoke when I stood and cross the room. "I have to go to the bathroom," he said. I decided to wait to say goodbye until he was finished – the doctors said he would have bad balance for a while, and I didn't want him to fall in my absence.

I started packing up some of my things (some work papers I showed him, a history book that I was reading a few pages aloud to him from every day) and after a few minutes he came back into the room. Instead of going back to bed, though, he stood at the huge bay windows for minute, looking down on the "white coat ghetto" neighborhood below. Nice little houses dotted the street, but were mostly invisible due to the neighborhood's healthy tree canopy.

"Huh," my dad said after a few minutes.

"What?"

"Oh I was just... one of those houses reminded me of one of the houses on our street right after your mother and I moved in."

"Oh, the house looks the same?"

My dad thought for a minute, then: "A little, but mostly the door." He pointed. I got up to look and saw that one of the houses down there had a bright orange front door. A "pop of color," no doubt.

He was already walking to get back to bed.

"Bill was helping us move into the house," he said, referring to his younger brother. "In 1980. I remember we were unloading a couch from a truck and he slipped and fell in the yard."

"Ow!" The rest of the couch fell to the ground, too. "You okay?" My dad asked Bill.

"Yeah, Butch," Uncle Bill said back, using my dad's hometown nickname. My mom was somewhere in the house unpacking one of the cardboard boxes. Bill had stumbled onto the lawn, lush from the rainy spring that had, of late, given way to prematurely sweltering summer. My dad put down his end of the couch and helped Bill back to his feet. My mom seemed not to have noticed, or not to have thought that her assistance was needed. But a middle-aged man, tall, balding, with a round and friendly face, was already halfway across the street to render aid. He saw that Bill had gotten back to his feet with no damage sustained, and the friendly man slowed his pace a little but continued forward, arm outstretched.

"Bob Shaw," he said, shaking my dad's hand and Bill's hand in turn. "We live right across the street," and he pointed at a healthy-looking white house. "Can I give ya a hand?"

"Ralph," my dad said, using his government name instead of his hometown alias. "And sure!" he smiled. The three of them carried the heavy sofa inside, into the living room. Mr. Shaw introduced himself to my mother, helped move a few more heavy things (dining room table, waterbed, relatively high-end stereo set), and accepted my dad's ubiquitous offer of a beer.

There was no front porch, and my dad wanted to be introduced to the general layout of the street, so they poured their beers into coffee mugs and set off down the sidewalk. Mr. Shaw introduced them to Mr. Pike (who had been the neighborhood watch captain during World War II, making sure everyone's lights were out at night so as to avoid German bombing raids), Mr. and Mrs. Pellet (who had been on the street when it was incepted), Mr. Morris (the town judge), and various others. Down at the end of the street, where it curved and went downhill before transforming into Roosevelt Drive, there was a bastard of a blue house, hidden behind overgrown hedges. I remember the place even now—darker than the rest of the houses; only the older kids would make an attempted trick or treat on Halloween (always unsuccessful). The lights were always off. The door was sort of shabby and sometimes off its hinges. The hedges, in 1980 and also later, in my youth, untrimmed and encroaching on the airspace above the sidewalk.

Back in 1980, though, Mr. Shaw pointed the place out to my dad. The hedges were already overgrown back then, but the house had yet to attain its creepy reputation. Bill, my dad, and Mr. Shaw walked up the multicolored stone walkway to the front door and Mr. Shaw knocked on the screen. The front door was open, so the first few feet of the cavernous entryway could be seen with what little of the bright afternoon sun could manage to penetrate.

"Larry?" Mr. Shaw asked. "It's Bob."

"Yeah, be right there," came a friendly reply from somewhere inside. After a minute or so, an extraordinarily ordinary-looking man came to the screen, opening it with his arm across the threshold in a welcoming manner.

"Larry, this is Ralph and his brother Bill. Ralph just moved into 303."

"Oh, well, welcome!" Larry exuded, shaking everyone's hands, even Mr. Shaw's. The whites of his eyes seemed to brighten, but the dark brown of the irises remained stubbornly opaque. "Oh and I see you've got some beverages; can I top you off? Gee, I'd have Sue come out to say hi, but she's feeling a little under the weather."

Bill and my dad both agreed that a top off was called for. Larry disappeared back into the house and came back out with a couple bottles of Genesee red eye. He poured a little bit into everyone's coffee mug, and kept the leftover liquid in a bottle for himself, while everyone stood around on the porch and chatted about the weather (unseasonably warm, and likely to stay that way for a while), the election (it was probably gonna be Carter and Reagan, believe it or not; when would Kennedy withdraw?), and local news (mafia car bombings were still going off in the city every so often).

Mr. Shaw was a great mediator of the conversation; he moved things along when they got stale and he provided much needed exposition when Larry got ahead of himself and forgot that Dad and Bill had no context for anything that had to do with Rochester. Larry was friendly, but a little too friendly. They were only talking to him for 10-15 minutes or so, but it was obvious that he relished the conversation, speaking a little too loudly, gesticulating a little too strongly, as if he hadn't had a front porch conversation for some time and had been saving up for it.

Everyone's coffee mugs or bottles eventually emptied, and my dad remembered that he should probably get back to his house and wife. "Thanks for the beer," he said, and Bill "yeah"d in agreement. "We should do it again soon."

"Oh, definitely!" Larry grinned. "Any time you see me out here in the yard or any time my door's open, just come knock and have a beer and a chat!"

"Good seein' you, Larry," Mr. Shaw said as he stepped off the porch. The three travelers got about halfway down the walkway when Larry stopped waving at them and closed his front door.

"Jeez," my dad remarked, looking back. The door was painted a bright, fluorescent orange, like a lifejacket.

"I know," Mr. Shaw said. "He painted it that way a few months ago. A couple of us talked about it and thought about mentioning it to him, but Sue, his wife, got sick a little while ago, and we figured he's a little hung up about the whole thing." The door, they'd assumed, had been an ill attempt at remaining cheerful.

Turns out Sue hadn't been seen in a few months, except for a couple "hey there"s from some of the concerned wives on the street. She looked well, but from her demeanor it was apparent that she was, in fact, not.

Bill and my dad said goodbye to Mr. Shaw at the front walkway. He went back across the street to his house. The afternoon had gotten stale and hazy. A mourning dove was off somewhere going, "ooo-OOh, ooo, ooo-ooo…" Dad and Bill went inside and unpacked an obligatory half-dozen or so boxes before it became acceptable to head down the street to the Hampshire House for some more drinks.

***

My dad and Larry never seemed to get together that summer to have that beer and chat. Dad got busy with his new job at Xerox, and when he was in the neighborhood, Larry never seemed to be outside. It was rare that his front door was open, and those occasions seemed never to coincide with my dad's availability.

No one saw much of Sue, either. Then came one day in mid-August when the street awoke to find that Larry's door was no longer the now-familiar fluorescent orange. That had been replaced with a cerulean blue, with some of the panels painted a pastel sky color, approaching white.

Come Autumn a delegation, my dad included, took it upon themselves to go over to Larry's house with some pie and beer. "Sure thing fellas," he said cheerily when they asked if he wanted to have a drink. But he didn't seem honest in his cheerfulness. "Just give me a few minutes and I'll be right out," he said through the screen door. Bob Shaw, my dad, and a couple others sat in some chairs on Larry's porch, looking at each other knowingly: the door had worried them. It looked like a light sky with clouds – it looked like nothing else in the neighborhood – it stood out – it looked like something a child would have for wallpaper.

They were almost finished with their first beers when Larry finally joined them. He seemed a little harried, but as soon as he opened one of the drinks and started talking, he seemed normal enough. They talked about Peter Gabriel and Rush, about Governor Carey, about some local sports news and predictions about the weather that coming fall. No one wanted to talk about Sue, least of all, it seemed, Larry. Neither he nor the others brought up the painted door, either. He never lost that sense of being rushed or stressed; before he finished his drink, he stood up and announced that he had some stuff to tend to in the house, but he assured everyone that he was grateful for the pie and the beer and the talk. He left the porch with assurances that they would have beer and chat sometime soon, for sure.

Once the delegation was walking back up the walkway, they began talking.

"He didn't say much, did he?" Bob Shaw asked. "A little quiet, I mean."

"Maybe he's down about Sue," suggested one of the neighbors. They all agreed to reach out to see if Larry needed any actual help with Sue, with house stuff, anything. Unfortunately, this agreement to reach out didn't last much longer than the time it took everyone to walk back to his respective home. Then their lives took over, and helping Larry was put on the mental backburner.

My dad went out in the backyard and listened to the wind blowing through the sugar maples. A bird was going, "pe-kew, pe-kew, troo-troo-troo, troo-troo-troo." He finished off another beer before going inside to watch the news.

After a few weeks, Larry's front door changed to a pinstripe pattern of hunter green, bubblegum pink, and deep brown.

***

Bob Shaw came knocking at my dad's door one Friday that autumn. The predawn sky was grey, and the crickets filled the neighborhood with "eeeeeeee."

Bob was still in his pajamas. My dad had put on some jeans before opening the door.

"I think Sue's gone," Bob said to my dad. "I wanted to get some people together to go talk to Larry. Maybe take him out for drinks today."

My dad thought about whether it would be O.K. to miss work, but then immediately pushed that thought out of his mind, "Yeah, sure."

A bunch of the neighbors went to go see Larry, who was sitting on his front porch. He wasn't crying, nor was he staring off or acting otherwise traumatized. He seemed almost normal. His smiles came either a little too quickly or a little late, as if forced and forgotten, and his voice wavered slightly, but that was all.

Bob, my dad, and a couple others went up the front walkway. "Larry," Bob started, "we're so sorry for your loss."

To my dad this line seemed cliche. But he couldn't think of anything better. So when he got to the porch and shook Larry's hand, he, too, said, "Sorry for your loss, Larry."

They sat down on the porch for a bit while the sun came up, then Bob left and came back with beers. They started drinking.

The day drew on, and the crowd eventually walked over to Hampshire House for more drinks. They toasted to Sue. Larry smiled at that. Finally they started walking back into the neighborhood, and it took a while before my dad realized that he and Larry were walking alone. There was a vague memory of Bob having been with them for most of the day, but someone, maybe his wife?, picked him up at the bar an hour or so ago. Maybe two or three.

Larry started talking to my dad,

"She was laying in the living room when I went down there this morning. It was still dark. She was awake though. She was in the kitchen, and fell, hit her head on the counter, and crawled into the living room.

"I called the ambulance and they got there pretty quick. She said she had to go upstairs and go to the bathroom, and I told her, 'Sue, we can't get you upstairs. You'll have to go right here and maybe I can bring a towel down or something.' And she goes, pretty loudly, 'No!'

"The medics asked her if her blood pressure was usually that low, and she told them it wasn't, before they put her in the ambulance and drove her to Strong Hospital. I forgot to say goodbye, but I guess I figured I'd be following them and would see her soon anyway."

Larry and my dad turned onto Bradford Street. The houses were dark. The grass was silvery with dew. My dad listened with growing nervousness.

"I got to the hospital and parked my car and went in. Someone at the front desk sort of directed me to where she would be. I turned the corner and they had her on a bed. Like a dozen doctors and nurses and technicians were surrounding her, and they were doing CPR. Her mouth was open.

"They asked me why she might have fluid in her abdomen, and I told them that I didn't know. The doctor said they would do everything until I told them not to. Her heart kept coming back when they gave her adrenalin, but then stopping again and they had to do CPR again. One of the nurses said, 'She likes the epi.'

"After a while, they kept doing CPR and the doctor sort of made it clear that it was just gonna prolong the inevitable. They said they could make her feel comfortable and I could say goodbye. So they gave her like eight times the normal morphine dose, took the tube out of her throat, and let me stand with her in the little bay.

"I held her hand and she was sort of breathing normally. Her eyes were closed. Then, with each slow breath, they opened a little and started looking up at the ceiling. She looked surprised. I didn't know if she was really conscious or not. I just kept holding her hand. Then after a minute, her eyes started to close a little, with each breath. She took a few breaths with her eyes closed. There were pauses in between, just like when she used to fall asleep on the couch..."

Larry looked down at the sidewalk for a bit, then they crossed Susquehanna Road and kept walking downhill towards the intersection where Larry's house was. My dad couldn't think of anything to say.

Larry went on, "She breathed a few times like that. Then she didn't breathe. And after a few seconds, I realized she was done breathing. The doctor came in and listened to her heart and said, 'I think she's passed.'

"I wasn't sure whether I was supposed to leave her there. The therapist person they had come talk to me eventually brought me into the bay next door so we could talk about cremation. I could smell that Sue had crapped herself, somewhere there in the end; I wonder if that made the therapist uncomfortable."

They were now walking in front of Larry's house. He wasn't crying. He seemed thoughtful.

They got to the front of the walkway and stopped. "Thanks for taking me out for drinks, Ralph," Larry said.

"Of course," my dad finally said. "Anytime, Larry." And Larry walked up his front walkway to his hideous door. He stopped to look at it for a moment before he went inside. My dad kept walking up the sidewalk towards his house. He heard a sound and realized that it was Larry banging around in his garage for some reason.

***

Pre-dawn. There was a loud THRUMMMMMM in the neighborhood that woke everyone up. At first, my mom and dad thought it was coming from somewhere in their house, but my dad looked out the window and saw Bob Shaw and a couple others on their front lawns. He went outside and heard that the sound was coming from somewhere down the street, towards Larry's house.

Bob and my dad and a couple others walked down to Larry's to see what it was.

The door was a dark purple, almost black. They looked at it and my dad realized that the thrumming noise was coming from the door itself. It was vibrating, pulsing, along with the sound. Each time it pulsated, black streaks came out from the middle, until after a minute or so the streaks were always there on the dark purple, swirling, swirling.

Larry was standing in front of the door. Bob Shaw shouted something to him, but my dad couldn't really understand it over the noise, so there was no way Larry could have understood. Larry realized, though, that there were people near his front lawn, because he turned and looked at them. His face was emotionless and empty.

He started walking towards the door. My dad and Bob Shaw reached out, even though they were across the yard and could not reach. Bob Shaw broke into a sprint. His head was low and his hands flat, slicing, like an olympic sprinter in profile. Larry touched the door as he stepped towards it. It sucked him in.

It took a second for my dad to realize that Larry hadn't walked through the doorway; he'd walked, slid, into the door itself. Like it was some sort of portal. Bob Shaw stopped running just before he got to the porch. It looked like a breeze was blowing what little hair there was on top of his head, towards the portal.

The THRUMMMM reached a lower pitch, like an engine straining uphill, and after ten seconds or so it stopped. It echoed. The echo died away. The neighborhood seemed impossibly quiet. Somewhere some bird was going "teu, teu, tweet-tweet.

Tweet-tweet."

***

I knew Bob Shaw as a tall, white-haired, kindly man who lived in the white house across the street. His wife, Mrs. Shaw, was short, and equally kindly, like the advertising mascot for some home product or baked good; I can't not picture her wearing a white apron and holding out a tray of cookies or something, even though I don't think that is an actual memory that I've ever had. The apron has little half-circle frills.

Their son, Sonny, was in high school when I was a toddler. His hair was movie-star shaggy. I fed the Shaws' cats when they were away. Years later, they left the neighborhood and retired to the Finger Lakes. My dad and some of my friends and I were down there for dinner, at the Switzerland Inn, when we saw the Shaws at a nearby table.

"Bob!" My dad called out, smiling. I was smiling too. Bob Shaw looked over at us and, after a moment, he smiled too. He stood and sauntered over, "Oh, it's my… neighbors!" He said, before shaking hands and greeting and talking and catching up.

As I sat in the hospital room and listened to my dad finish his story, I thought about that pause. I always thought that Bob Shaw maybe just didn't know how to refer to us. Ex-neighbors? Former across-the-street-people? Now, though, there was more to think about in that pause. He wasn't searching for a word to describe my dad; he was hiding one and settling on another.

My dad started again, "that house was always the scary one for Halloween. With the lights off. Do you remember?" I told him I did.

"We should have-" my dad started, before sort of shaking his head and closing his eyes. Then his eyes opened again, "We didn't-" and he shook his head again, dismissing the thought entirely. "I think I'm gonna go to sleep."

I said O.K. and closed down the laptop on which we had been watching the movie. I headed down the hallway and down the elevators and out the door and onto the street and I looked up at the big glass building where most of the lights were off. I could see my dad's room. I thought about Larry and the portal.

ABOUT THE AUTHOR

Bo Shoemaker is a trail runner and history run leader. In his spare time, he practices law in Western New York.